ReMIND

Scott McElhaney

Life is 10% what happens to you and 90% how you react to it.

Charles R. Swindoll

PROLOGUE- Effect and Cause

"If I had it all to do over again…"

Seriously! I have to ask – how many people on the planet have uttered a phrase that started with those very words just this week alone? Actually, let's take this a little further! How many times *a day* does someone on Earth begin a statement with those same exact words? And then let's ask ourselves this - why do they start the phrase that way? Most likely it's because something life-altering had just come about that insisted upon a firm self-evaluation.

"If I had it all to do over again…"

And that self-evaluation is naturally going to lead their thoughts backward through time, bouncing from one important event to another. Sifting backward, you realize that the life you have now is the ultimate and final effect of a bunch of causes. Cause-and-effect in the original course of events… or effect and cause as you look backward from the viewpoint of the final effect. Tracing back, you'll move from effect to cause, effect to cause, effect to cause until finally you discover that single event that started it all.

My event, the one that should have killed me, happened on a hot summer day back when I had just turned nineteen years old. If I wouldn't have jumped off that bridge into the lake at the Firestone Country Club, who knows what would have come of my life? If I hadn't joined my friends, sliding down that mossy dam and into that nasty creek below, everything in my life would have most certainly turned out differently.

But alas, my friends and I had jumped off that bridge and into the lake dozens of times that day. And then we each sat at the top of that concrete dam which was meant to keep that circular manmade lake from exceeding a certain maximum flood level. We slid down that fifteen-foot dam and splashed into the stagnant pool at the bottom. All of this occurred beneath that same bridge that we had initially leapt from. We climbed back up that hill, walked to the middle of the bridge again, and then jumped into the lake over and over again. That bridge and the dam served as a poor kid's water park on a hot summer's day. But that particular hot summer's day was the day that changed it all.

By the time we had hopped into the back of the pickup truck and headed home, I had somehow inhaled or aspirated something microscopic called Naegleria Fowleri or as it's more commonly known, a brain-eating amoeba for which there is no known cure.

If I had it all to do over again… well, before I answer that, perhaps I should tell you my story. My name is Donner Michaels and this is my story – a series of causes with some very interesting and curious effects. And as unreal and fantastic as it may all seem, please keep in mind that this is all true. Let me tell you about the guy who agreed to be a part of ReMIND.

PROLOGUE - Death Sentence

Wait, I'm not ready for chapter one just yet. Chapter one is going to begin where I woke up for the first time after… wait, I'm getting ahead of myself. So anyway, I guess I'm still in the prologue or prelude. I need to make sure you understand what all transpired to get me to the point that everything changed forever.

That fateful swim had happened during the summer after high school graduation. It had been me and my two best friends, David and "Bogey". Steve was Bogey's real name, but since he pronounced his S's as Sh's, he shounded a lot like Humphrey Bogart, shweetheart – hence Bogey.

Bogey had joined the Navy immediately following graduation, but he somehow managed to make it home for a few days in late July after boot camp. David already had one of those nice Monday-through-Friday jobs at a local call center, so he always had his weekends free. I, on the other hand, had just been promoted to shift supervisor at the Ponderosa Steakhouse where I'd worked since my junior year of high school. As such, my shift varied and I was currently logging almost fifty hours a week, oftentimes only getting one day off per week.

The planets had somehow all aligned to allow the three of us to be off work and in Akron on that particular Saturday in late July. Fate, as well as the intense 95-degree heat, insisted upon a day at our favorite unorthodox and perhaps illegal water park. And because of that, I was given a death sentence, although I didn't know about it at that time.

Ten days would pass before the headaches were intense enough to warrant a hospital visit. I'd arrived at the emergency room around six AM, and by ten o'clock, I'd been informed that thanks to a brain-eating amoeba known as N. Fowleri, I had about a week to ten days left to live. They pulled no punches and apologetically informed me that I was most certainly going to die in spite of the intense antibiotic regimen they intended to put me on. As you could imagine, my entire family was in shock and devastated by the news, as was I. But that wasn't the end of my story. No, that was still actually just part of this elongated prologue. I haven't even given you chapter one yet! Try to keep up!

PROLOGUE - Large Hadron Collider

After a pretty bland hospital lunch of lukewarm macaroni and cheese and a burned slice of garlic bread, I was visited by a skeletal old man with dark skin who identified himself as Doctor Ahmad Khayyat. He informed me that he had just rushed over from the Cleveland Clinic when he caught wind about my case. He spoke in quick bursts of Arabic-accented sentences that were sometimes hard to follow. But by the end of his introduction, I believed that he happened to be an award-winning surgeon who specialized in a very experimental version of Alzheimer's recovery that he called ReMIND.

I'm embarrassed now to admit that I laughed at him when he said that. After all, everyone knows that there's no such thing as recovery from Alzheimer's. And to make matters worse, I hadn't been diagnosed with that particular disease. As a matter of fact, I was still probably at least forty years shy of the early-onset version of his specialty. That was when he felt the need to be more heartless and direct.

"You are in the same grave situation as a person with Alzheimer's except yours is going to progress at a hundred… no, a thousand times faster. You need to give me an answer *today* or I will not be able to help you. I need an answer yesterday as a matter of fact!" he said in hard-to-understand English.

"What's this entail?" I asked, trying to make myself comfortable in that crunchy hospital bed.

The man was looking very impatient as he crossed his arms.

"We really don't have time to discuss it. I need you while you still have a brain. Tell me now!" he almost shouted.

"Yes!" I blurted, "Save my life if you can!"

And just like that, I signed a few e-Docs on his tablet and then I was rushed off to about ten different areas of that hospital. I might have had an MRI or perhaps a CT scan. I was injected with dyes and heard terms that I didn't understand such as myelogram (and no, I don't know if I spelled it correctly). For all I know, I was wheeled through the heart of a nuclear reactor as well as the Large Hadron Collider in Switzerland. It's all a blur to me in hindsight, but I can tell you that when I was wheeled back to my room that evening, I was exhausted.

My exhaustion didn't stop them from injecting me with stuff every hour or two. Throughout it all, my parents and siblings kept me company. David even managed to pay me a visit as well as a few people from Ponderosa Steakhouse. But by eight o'clock however, I'm ashamed to admit that I finally crashed hard.

PROLOGUE - Emergency Coma

I awoke at two AM as I was suddenly getting wheeled from my room by a group of several nurses or doctors who seemed a little too harried or frantic for my liking. I commented on this as I struggled to hide my eyes from the bright lights in the hallway.

"What's the emergency?" I grumbled, "My head still hurts the same as it did yesterday. It's not gotten worse."

That was the moment when Dr. Khayyat came into view. He had been escorting my moving bed apparently. He held a file in his hand which he seemed to be examining as he walked briskly to my right.

"Temporal, parietal, and occipital are completely intact and I absolutely need those if we're to beat this, Donner. Your claustrum is still available, so we need to move quickly," he spoke in his broken English, "We must go to South America tonight if ReMIND is to be a success."

"*South America*?" I laughed.

"Tonight!" he agreed, "You will be put into a medically-induced coma for the time being, so you won't experience much of the journey. Listen, though. Are you listening to me?"

I turned to that skeletal doctor, "Yes, I'm listening."

"Good. When you wake from this coma, you will be at our experimental ReMIND facility in South America. If all goes as planned, and I'm confident it will, when you wake up, you will already be on the road to recovery."

"Seriously?" I breathed.

"I already told you that I'm the one who can cure Alzheimer's. You are going to witness firsthand that I take the impossible and I reverse it. Welcome to my world, Donner."

As I look back now, I don't believe I was even out of the hallway before I fell asleep… or went into a coma.

ONE

I awoke to the sound of seagulls and the rolling ocean surf. I only recognized such a sound because my family and I had spent a week at Myrtle Beach shortly after graduation. Being a kid from Ohio who had no prior experience with the ocean, those first few nights were spent believing that there was a ferocious storm outside our hotel balcony. It had truly sounded like raging winds and a constant downpour out there all night long and into the morning. It was only once I'd opened that balcony door the following morning that I discovered that those watery sounds didn't always have to mean wind and rain. By the third night, I learned to love the sound of that rolling ocean surf.

I opened my eyes to discover that I had been lying in a large and unfamiliar bed, not unlike those large queen-size beds at the Myrtle Beach hotel. I sat up quickly, noticing right away that my head didn't hurt anymore. The next thing that I noticed was the reason why I had woken up hearing the surf and the seagulls so clearly. To my immediate right was a sliding glass door that had been left open, allowing that salty warm breeze to enter the already warm hotel room.

Hotel room…

That was, after all, what the room appeared to be. Those two tropical paintings on the wall with the giant television centered between them near the foot of the bed reminded me of the Beachfront Marriott. To my left was a miniature marble counter with a microwave oven, an air fryer, and a coffee maker on it. Beneath that counter was a fairly large 'mini' fridge with a small freezer door at the top.

I looked to my right again to gaze upon that open glass sliding door with the drawn curtains. Between my bed and that door was a small beige sofa, a wooden coffee table, and a laptop computer that was currently plugged in. The ongoing call of the seagulls beckoned me to pay a visit to that open door.

I drew the thin white covers back, discovering right away that I was wearing a set of soft cotton gingham-print pajamas that had probably gone out of style even before my own parents were born. Since I was still apparently a patient, I disregarded that thought and slid quickly out of bed.

Patient…

Hospital…

No matter how you looked at it, this clearly wasn't a hospital, yet I was confident that I was most certainly still a patient. I'd just had emergency experimental surgery that apparently was a success. My head didn't hurt, and I currently had to assume that I was in South America somewhere.

I approached the sliding glass door which had offered me passage to a high concrete balcony with a decorative black metal railing. Beyond said railing were those many seagulls that had been pretty much hovering in front of my neighbor's balcony. I could see tiny portions of food being tossed into the air and being caught in the beaks of those talented and greedy birds.

I stepped out onto the balcony, welcoming that warm ocean breeze. I took two steps and then took hold of that metal railing as I breathed in that wonderful salty scent. The bright sun was hovering just an inch above that spot where the ocean met the sky by my current reckoning. If I were to compare that horizon to that of my Myrtle Beach vacation, then I'd guess it was anywhere from six to six-thirty in the morning. But again, I really didn't know where I was, so it was truly just an uneducated estimate.

"Mornin'!" a man called from my left.

A concrete wall offered privacy for each of our balconies, but that didn't prevent my newly discovered neighbor from leaning forward while he clutched his railing. I could only see his head and left shoulder. This was an elderly gentleman with thinning gray hair and a wide smile as sincere as that bright morning sun.

"Hi, I'm Donner. I'm… I just woke up," I said, moving toward him and offering my hand.

He reached a hand around that concrete barrier and shook mine. The hungry seagulls weren't giving that guy any peace even though he had taken a moment to greet his neighbor.

"Earl," he said, "I hate to be so forward and abrupt, but I'm mighty surprised to meet someone your age here!"

"My age?" I pondered aloud for a moment before the thought occurred to me, "Wait! Alzheimer's... Are you a patient of Doctor Khayyat?"

"*Was* a patient! Come on, buddy. We love to use those past-tense words here. Did Doctor Khayyat help you as well?" he asked, "Even early-onset doesn't affect people your age, I'm fairly certain."

"I was a unique prize for the good doctor apparently," I shrugged, leaning on the railing as I looked over at him, "Brain-eating amoeba. I guess you don't typically come across many cases early enough where the brain isn't already half-gone."

"Wow! You're right about that! N. Fowleri usually shows symptoms in about two to fifteen days. And after that, you're probably dead in three to seven days. How'd he find you in time?" he asked.

I couldn't help but to arch my eyebrow when he used the medical term for my disease. Probably 99.9 percent of the population couldn't tell you the medical term for my death sentence. The man chuckled when he saw my expression.

"*Doctor* Earl Robbins," he inserted, "Retired neurosurgeon. So yes, I can appreciate what you've been through as well as these many successful cures around here from Alzheimer's. I hate to be the bearer of bad news, but I'm afraid that you are currently residing inside a nursing home full of people who are all probably three to four times your age, son."

"Nursing home?" I laughed aloud, "Come on! This place is surely a fancy hotel!"

"Isn't it though? I suppose it's part of the reward for allowing ourselves to be experimented on," he laughed as well, "How about you join me for breakfast? My treat!"

"Breakfast?"

"Is everything going to end in a question mark with you?" he groaned, "Meet me in the hallway outside our... outside our *hotel* rooms."

I breathed out a long sigh as I looked over at the elderly man. Finally, after a moment of hesitation, I nodded and then he smiled. It was time to get some answers.

TWO

Earl had been right to warn me. By the time the hostess seated us in the hotel restaurant (I refused to think of it as a nursing home just yet), I started to realize the stares that I was getting. There wasn't a single person in the entire restaurant beneath the age of seventy. Yeah, I couldn't confirm this number, but even if I were wrong, I wasn't more than a year or two off. I might as well have been getting seated inside a Bob Evans or Cracker Barrel. I clearly didn't belong and it was making me feel a little uncomfortable.

"If this is a nursing home, where's the staff? I guess I'm asking about who I'd report to in order to ask if I could leave and go home," I whispered across the table.

Earl chuckled and shook his head, "Ignore the stares, Donner. If they knew what you'd been cured of, they'd be as amazed as I am. Stop acting so uncomfortable."

"Were they all cured of Alzheimer's?" I asked.

He nodded, "Most likely. That or various other diseases of progressive neurological deterioration. It seems to be Doctor Khayyat's main area of focus, even in your case."

That was all I needed to hear in order to motivate me to do what I had done next. I clutched the edge of the table and then scooted out my chair as I abruptly stood up and looked around the room.

I cleared my throat, "Doctor Khayyat freed me from a brain-eating amoeba. I'm sorry that I can't relate, but I *can* relate to a fast-forwarded brain destroying disease that kills its host in *days* instead of years. Sorry that I'm merely nineteen if that offends anyone."

I sat back down as the many audible whispers began to fill the room. Earl didn't seem to be very pleased with my abrupt announcement. Soon, however, we started getting visits from various people. One-by-one, these elderly people introduced themselves to me. By the time the waitress took our order, I had probably met at least a dozen other people. I couldn't recall a single name however, but I was glad to see that they didn't view me as an enemy infiltrator.

"Did you notice anything odd about any of those who came over to meet you?" Earl asked, taking a drink from his steaming cup of coffee.

I shook my head, tearing open a packet of sugar to add to my tea, "They're all old enough to be my grandparents?"

"Sure, I'll give you that. And don't forget that these are all the ones who were slowly losing touch with reality. Myself included, of course. But what seems to be missing in this entire room?" he asked, "Keep in mind their elderly state."

Without trying to be obvious, I casually glanced around the room. I looked for the subtle things like hats, glasses, and purses. Nothing seemed to be extraordinary.

"Canes or walkers," he finally offered, "These people you see all around us are exceptionally healthy. Doctor Khayyat did a little more than improve their brain function. So please don't disregard these people as a bunch of old geezers in a nursing home."

I laughed a little too loudly at that statement. Several heads turned in our direction.

"How bad off were you?" I asked.

He nodded subtly, "Really bad from what I can remember. But keep in mind that none of us ever got to witness the worst part. We had all been taken before it got too bad. But I can tell you that I had sufficient hip problems at the time and I often used a walker to get around. I can't explain it but I feel twenty years younger and I obviously don't use a walker anymore."

As I glanced around the room, it was easy to confirm that these people did truly seem to be exceptionally healthy and energetic. Even those who were probably in their nineties were laughing and conversing with vigor and pep.

"How big is this place? I mean, have you ever taken a guess at how many people Doctor Khayyat rescued?" I asked.

"*Rescued*," he repeated, "I like that. I've been here about a month and in that time, I've probably met or seen about a hundred others. If you think about it though, we're on the top floor of a four-story building. Unless they decide to build another nursing home, we might not see too many other people arriving. I think there are only three or four more empty suites left."

"You've been here a month?" I groaned just as the waitress returned with our food.

I paused while she set down our plates and refilled our drinks. Earl had chosen two eggs sunny side up with bacon. I had selected the biscuits and sausage gravy which looked amazing. Once the waitress left, I then leaned toward Earl.

"You've been here a *month*? How long are we required to stay after we've been cured? I want to go home! My parents probably want to see me and I'm sure they want to know how I'm doing!" I whispered.

"You can still communicate with them using the laptop in your room. I talk to my daughter every day! We've got no cell service, but the internet works just fine. No Wi-Fi however, but I've always said that the internet is faster and more reliable using those cables anyway. Actually, you might even want to reach out to your parents soon to let them know how you're feeling!"

I cut up my biscuits, then I showered my breakfast with salt and pepper. I then forked a bite and shoved it into my mouth without regard to the temperature. It was exceptionally hot, so it took me a moment to carefully chew it up and swallow it. It was as good and spicy as I'd hoped.

"What about landlines? I'd really prefer to call them if it's all the same," I said, "I'm not even sure I know their email addresses."

"No, it's not an email connection. When you signed up for the surgery, you were given a special Text-mail account. Your family was already given your Text-mail address and your own personal account here was already populated with their information. It actually links to their cell phones," he explained, "All this should already be on your laptop."

I was getting impatient with this guy's lack of answers. Surely he realized that I still wanted to know why he'd been here a full month and how long we were required to stay. Sure, as beautiful as that beach was beneath my balcony, I wasn't in any hurry, but I'd also like to know if this was a year-long commitment.

"Earl," I sighed, "How long are we required to stay?"

"Well, I'm sure each individual case is different. A lot of it is based on these experimental ReMIND drugs they need to keep us on and for how long. Since none of these meds are FDA approved, you couldn't be taking them anymore if you returned home to the US," he explained, "Remember, even Doctor Khayyat's experimental surgeries weren't approved, so that's why we had to leave the country in the first place."

"So wait… this isn't a permanent fix? We need to continue doing something in order to make sure it doesn't come back?" I asked.

"Didn't you read the papers before signing them?" he asked.

"No, I didn't have time. He said I needed to give him an answer immediately."

Earl shook his head, adding more pepper to his eggs. I took another bite of my food.

"I'm sorry if this is all coming as a surprise to you. I'd recommend talking to your doctor when you see her later today," he said, "Or actually… looks like she's headed our way right now."

I turned to look in the direction of his gaze. I was startled… no, I was *stunned* by the South American dark-haired supermodel headed toward us with a wide smile on her face. She most certainly wasn't a doctor just judging by the facial perfection and the perfect curves of her body. Although I guess she could have certainly been a doctor on your typical afternoon soap opera.

"Donner Michaels?" she said, blinding me with that bright smile as she stuck out her hand, "You woke sooner than I'd expected! You saw that I left your balcony door open to give you a welcome greeting when you rose. I'm Doctor Coral Laekin, but everyone just calls me Laekin. We keep it casual here. So, how are you feeling? How's the head?"

I shook her hand as she invited herself to sit down in the vacant seat to my left.

"I'm... I'm fine. Laekin, do you mind if I ask what this place is and how long do I have to stay? I actually have a million questions."

She gestured toward the restaurant entrance behind her, "Not a problem! I'm here to make your stay as pleasant as possible however this isn't where we should discuss it. My office is just outside of the restaurant, then down the hall to the right. You'll see my name on the door. Come see me after breakfast."

I was about to say something when she stood up abruptly and excused herself from the table. I turned to Earl who merely shrugged. I then thumbed toward that woman as she quickly headed away.

"Is she real? There ain't no way she's a doctor! She can't be more than twenty-five and she clearly belongs in fashion magazines or on TV!"

"*Thirty*-five actually and yes, she's quite real. It's not her fault she's so beautiful, so don't hold it against her," Earl replied.

I shook my head as I watched the elderly man seated in front of me. I couldn't understand how he was so casual about everything.

"Well, I'm not sure I can keep from gawking at her while I talk to her."

He laughed, then gestured toward my plate, "I'm sure she's used to it. Hurry up and eat if you want to catch her in her office."

THREE

"Doctor Laekin?" I hollered after knocking just beneath her nameplate.

"Come on in, Donner," I heard her call from the other side of that sturdy wooden door.

I had wondered just then if the door would open up into a waiting room when I pushed on it. But once I'd done that, I was quick to discover that it hadn't. I immediately found myself inside a nice little wood-paneled office. The lovely doctor was currently seated behind a large mahogany desk that happened to be flanked by bookshelves on the wall behind her to the right and left. I noticed just then that she had been watching me as I examined her office.

"My credentials are posted on the wall behind me. You'll learn to trust me over time, my friend," she smiled at me as she gestured toward the chair in front of her desk, "Please, close the door and have a seat."

"It's not a lack of trust, Doctor," I said, closing the door behind me, "I'm just feeling a bit overwhelmed currently. Earl said that I'm not able to call my parents and it's also sounding like I'm not even allowed to leave this place."

"I'm sorry, and please call me Laekin. I want you to feel comfortable enough to come to me with any concerns or questions you have," she said, watching me as I sat down in the comfortable chair across from her, "I read your file and I noticed that yours was a very hurried affair. Everyone else probably had plenty of time to examine all the details before signing up, but you... I really must apologize."

I nodded, letting her see that I accepted her apology. I found myself unable to look at her simply because she might have actually been too beautiful. I never thought there could be such a thing, but even those bee-stung lips had me thinking about things I shouldn't.

"Well, can you just let me know about everything that I'd signed up for? How long am I here for and am I allowed visitors? And let's just get real - where is 'here' exactly?"

"No problem! We're just south of Rio de Janeiro in Brazil. This is a private beach owned solely by a private donor who has been funding Doctor Khayyat's research from the very beginning. Needless to say, this private donor had a lot of money and was genetically predisposed to developing Alzheimer's later in life. So, first and foremost, please enjoy yourself while you're here. You don't have to worry about tourists or vagrants on our lovely beach."

"Thank you. I do believe I'll make myself comfortable out there soon enough," I offered in an effort to show her that I wasn't as hostile as I truly felt currently deep down.

"And as far as visitors go, I'm going to have to ask my supervisors about that. And in regards to your other question… well, for now, I cannot accurately say how long you will need to stay here because we are fighting to allow this research to proceed further in the United States. We've shared the results, but we're simply not getting the sort of favor we expected. And the sort of nano-tech ReMIND drugs that we're using to improve the brain and keep the disease, or amoeba in your case, at bay are currently prohibited in the US even on an experimental level," she said, "Sure, there's plenty of nano-tech medicine trials going on in the US, but there are certain things about ours which are still prohibited by the closed-minded FDA. But we're still fighting to pave a way."

"So, until these drugs are approved, even for experimental use, we're all stuck down here in Rio?" I asked, "And are these medications something we will have to rely on for the rest of our lives?"

"Yes, the treatments are required in order to maintain this success. And I assure you that we are fighting to get these approved for use in the US. Until then, I do apologize, but yes, you're right in the assumption that you will not be allowed to return to the US if you wish to live," she explained, quite matter of fact.

I felt my shoulders slump at the realization of this. I wondered just then if my decision would have changed had I known I'd be indefinitely banished from my country, my friends, and my family.

"Well, how often do we require this illegal drug? If it's a weekly thing, then-"

"It's a nightly injection taken between dinner and bedtime," she interrupted, "Even missing a single dose could prove fatal. Basically, once those nanites repaired the brain, they require constant replenishment. But rest assured, you will never have to pay for this drug since you signed on as an experimental test subject. I think we both can appreciate the sort of money such a necessary drug is going to cost the consumer in the future."

"You're continually breaking my heart over and over again, Laekin. I'm going to be stuck at what appears to be a nice beach resort with… well, with a bunch of old people with whom I'll have nothing in common. I won't find a single peer amongst them."

"Well, as long as I'm not busy with another patient, you can always come talk to me," she offered.

I chuckled, then shook my head, "I can barely even look at you, much less hang out with you. I guess my only concern is, where do I report for my daily injections?"

"You can barely look at me? You know what? I'd been wanting to ask you about that. Why won't you look at me, Donner? You're so focused on my desk."

I quickly looked up from her desk and made a point to look at her, "I can look at you. I just choose not to."

"And why's that? As I already told you, you can feel comfortable talking to me."

"It's not something I'm prepared to talk about. Could I please be excused?"

"You're always free to come and go as you please. And to answer your question, Donner. No need to seek us out for your injections. We'll make sure to come find you. Just simply relax a little and enjoy what we've got here for you."

I merely shook my head as I rose from the chair, "Thank you, Laekin."

"I really hope you'll loosen up. Maybe next time you and I can go for a stroll."

FOUR

As I made my way up to the fourth floor, I made small talk on the elevator with a compact old woman with a snow white bouffant. That's all it would ever be in this curious new world – small talk. Even when I was visiting my grandparents, we really had nothing much to talk about besides family matters.

Edna was her name and she got off on the third floor. She insisted that I have a nice day and then she told me to watch out for Piper. I asked what she meant by that and she merely told me I'd understand full well when the time came. She promised me the time would come. She repeated that word again, then the elevator door closed.

"Piper?" I muttered to myself as I rode the elevator to my floor, "Sounds like the name of a bird."

When the elevator door opened, I was faced with two shirtless old men who had some bright neon-colored body boards tucked under their arms. I paid them both a smile as I slipped between them.

"Gonna be some pretty good waves today if you want to join us, kid," one of the men offered.

"Maybe later! Thanks!" I said, then I turned back to them as a thought came to mind, "Is there a place around here where I can get some swim trunks and a body board of my own?"

"Yeah, your closet!" the age-spotted bald guy said with a laugh, "Look forward to seeing you!"

The elevator door closed before I had a chance to clarify. I turned around and headed back to my room. Thankfully, all these rooms had names on the doors instead of room numbers. Once I approached my door, I noticed a little black glass screen just above the handle that simply read "Thumb". I pressed my thumb to that screen, then I heard a click. I twisted the knob to find that the door was unlocked.

I opened the door to discover a bright and wonderfully warm suite. The warmth was due to the fact that I'd accidentally left my curtains open as well as the balcony door. The air-conditioning couldn't fight off such a constant tropical breeze. The placement of the sun over that sparkling blue ocean also served to light up my whole suite.

The door shut behind me while I took notice of the closet to my immediate left. I opened it to discover some jackets, a couple of dressy suits, and a long trench coat hanging on the bar to the right. And right there on the left side of the closet was none other than a full-size white surf board, a yellow body board, two giant beach towels, two pairs of swim trunks, and a sturdy wooden beach umbrella. Doctor Khayyat apparently wanted us to enjoy ourselves as much as possible during our unintended incarceration. For that, I had to give him some kudos.

I actually found myself smiling as I closed that closet and headed over to the sofa. The laptop was still situated on the coffee table and I noticed just then that it had been an internet cord that was plugged into the device. Originally I had assumed that cord was the charger when I had caught a glimpse of it earlier today. It was only when I lifted the laptop from the coffee table that I discovered the unusual charger embedded into the tabletop. Apparently there was power somehow going through that table and into a protruding plug on the center of the table. The laptop had been resting firmly onto that plug this entire time.

I drew the portable computer onto my lap as I sat down on that comfortable sofa. I hit a random key, bringing the computer out of its sleep mode. The unfamiliar screen offered me several icons. One was labeled "Internet" although it didn't look like the familiar icons for Chrome, Firefox, or Explorer. The other icons were labeled "Games", "YouTube", "Music", "Desktop", "App Store", "Movies", and finally "Text-mail".

I immediately reached out and tapped the "Text-mail" icon. The screen instantly switched over to a sort of welcome screen. Below the welcome, it offered me contact icons for "Dad", "Mom", "Mom & Dad", "Brett" my brother, "Anna" my sister, and "Grandma" for my only surviving grandparent. Unfortunately, there were no icons for my friends. I figured I'd get those eventually. First and foremost, I wanted to reach out to my parents.

I clicked "Mom & Dad" and immediately began typing: "Hey Mom and Dad! I'm alive and well and I mean that in the best possible way. The headaches are gone and they tell me I'm cured, but unfortunately I'm stuck here near Rio de Janeiro due to a constant need for some weird drugs that aren't allowed in the US. They're working on changing that though. You wouldn't believe how many people Khayyat's experimental ReMIND surgeries have cured. These people are not only cured of Alzheimer's, they are vibrant and energetic. You should seriously see them. Two guys just passed me in the hall on their way out to go body-boarding in the surf! I doubt that either were under the age of eighty! My neighbor believes there are at least a hundred of us who are enjoying the benefits of Khayyat's miraculous efforts,

"But at the same time, I'm concerned about a few things. I won't burden you with any of that. I do, however, need you to satisfy my usual paranoia. I need to know that it's truly my real parents receiving this message. For that, I need to ask Dad this question. You said something to me in the car on the way to school in the sixth grade. It was a request that we both have often laughed about and no one else, not even Mom knows about it. Please reply with what that was. I love you both and hope to hear from you soon! Love, Donner."

I hit send, then noticed the little warning at the bottom of the page. Apparently texts would be sent in 160-character increments, so any long conversations would show up as a multiple spam text. Ultimately, that didn't matter to me. I'd have sent all that either way.

I clicked the icon that enabled audible alerts, then I returned the computer to its tabletop charger. I looked down at my clothing and discovered that I'd still been wearing my pajamas. Thank God about half the people at breakfast were dressed the same way. While that may have been natural for these old folks, it certainly wasn't natural for me. I wasn't about to start thinking of this place as a true nursing home.

I rose from the sofa and decided to check out the clothing options in that dresser beneath the enormous TV. Sure enough, I had been given enough summer clothing to get me through the rest of my life. I selected a pair of exceptionally long cargo shorts, a plain blue t-shirt, and a pair of flip flops. I wasted no time changing out of my pajamas and into more appropriate clothes. Afterward, I tossed my pajamas onto the corner of my bed. I wasn't sure what to do with my dirty clothes at the moment, so it seemed the best thing to do for the time being.

That was when I received a chirp from my laptop. I rushed over to the sofa and retrieved the laptop once more as I heard another chirp. I tapped the screen, bringing it out of sleep mode. All the icons were blurred behind the notification that my parents had responded. I tapped the accept icon.

"Donner, it's great to hear from you! And yes, in order to ease your paranoia, on the way to school that day, I told you that I really didn't want to go to work and that if you happened to go to the school nurse and claimed to be sick around ten AM, I really wouldn't be upset. And wouldn't you know that at a little after ten, I got a call at work from the school nurse. It's really me, Donner! I'm so glad to hear that the experiment was a success! Your mother and I are literally in tears right now. We worried that we'd never hear from you again! Please, describe everything to us. Tell us about your new home! Tell us everything! We love you too!"

I had tears in my own eyes at the moment. For some reason, I hadn't expected an exact and detailed explanation over what happened that day before school. I had somehow expected a vague response, proving to me that something fishy was going on. Instead, my dad told me exactly what had happened that morning. This was all for real and I was truly speaking with my parents.

I typed a quick reply to let them know all about my 'hotel room' and the delicious food. I told them about the beautiful view from my balcony. I shared everything that I'd experienced thus far. Then I asked them to keep my room and my stuff because I was fairly certain that I'd return again soon. I expected that these positive results would make national news eventually. Whether the FDA agreed or not, the public would have something to say, especially when their grandparents were still dying of this horrible disease back home.

    After I hit send, I decided that it was time to get out there and explore this new world. It was time to take advantage of the beautiful world I had just shared with my parents.

FIVE

I wasn't in the mood to go swimming just yet, but I did figure it was high time to go for a walk on the beach just to check it out. I took the elevator down to the ground floor, then I made my way through the lobby, past the restaurant, and out through the rear exit. Immediately past those glass double doors was a giant concrete patio that offered several reclining lawn chairs, a few rocking chairs, and four round glass top tables shaded under some colorful umbrellas. About a half-dozen people had already taken up residency out here on the patio this sunny morning.

I offered a few "good mornings" as I navigated around those reclining lawn chairs and then down the three stairs that led straight to the wooden boardwalk. Up until this point, I could still readily envision that hotel as being a nursing home based on its clientele both inside and out. Even as I looked down the length of the boardwalk, it was only the elderly I saw out talking a stroll.

I decided to head down the boardwalk toward my right since it appeared that there were several interesting places in that direction. The first place that caught my eye was the little ice cream stand with its tiny umbrella-covered tables scooted up alongside the boardwalk. No one seemed to be in the mood for ice cream this early in the day, but the quaint little booth remained open nonetheless.

Further down the boardwalk was a non-franchised seafood restaurant which also seemed to be open in spite of the early hour. I passed that by only to find myself pondering the wares of several little storefronts connected together like a miniature tourist plaza. The first storefront was a place that specialized in trinkets and souvenirs. Then the next store was clearly just your basic little convenience store that preyed on the snack-hungry. A spinner rack filled with a variety of seasoned potato chips was parked just outside the open door. Then the next store specialized in beach items such as snorkels, flip flops, inflatables, towels, swim masks, and everything in between. Beyond that was a cute little candy store straight from the 1950's.

After that plaza, I saw something that startled me. This little hole-in-the-wall bar looked entirely out of place. It was a blue cinderblock building painted with cartoonish sea life and sunken ships. Above the door, the word "SHIPWRECK" was painted to look like the letters were formed from broken boards. In the window to the left of the door were neon signs for Bud Light and Budweiser. In the window to the right, there were neon signs for Lite, Heineken, and Miller Genuine Draft. I then noticed a circular plastic lighted sign in the corner of that left window announcing "Billiards". This just seemed so out of place on a private beach intended for senior citizens recovering from Alzheimer's. I couldn't imagine these people being willing to blur those newly clear minds with alcoholic beverages.

"Do you play?" I heard a seductive voice ask from behind me.

"Play?" I asked, turning toward the slender and elegant woman behind me.

When one imagines the sort of people who would take up residency inside a typical nursing home, this lady wasn't what came to mind. Here was a tall, thin, and graceful-looking woman who wore a bright yellow sun dress that accentuated her curiously unrealistic curves. She was most certainly someone in her early to mid-sixties and she couldn't hide that fact no matter how much she had fought it. It was fairly evident that she fought off those years by regularly working out in the gym, or her neck, arms, shoulders, and legs wouldn't have looked so toned and muscular. I was also equally certain that this sturdy woman fought off those years by getting multiple breast implants, causing those unrealistically large mounds to strain against that dress while bulging from the top.

In spite of her efforts to hold onto her youth, she seemed content to keep that natural silvery gray hair. It looked good on her however because she kept it cut in a high and short style like many people my own age might have done. Actually, her hairstyle reminded me a lot of Billy Idol's hair. This wouldn't work for most elderly women, but when you were lucky enough to have the thin regal stature of this woman, it most certainly worked. I'd bet that she had a lot of propositions from the men in that nursing home and I was proud of her for that. This made me smile as she seemed to examine me.

"Yes, *play*. Do you play pool?" she asked, nodding her head toward the bar.

"Oh!" I chuckled, then nodded, "Yes, I've played it several times and I love it. But sadly, I'm not very good at it."

"Good, because neither am I! Would you care to escort a lady into the Shipwreck? I would sure like to spend some time playing pool with someone who doesn't sink the eight-ball on the break," she said, holding out her hand toward me.

I didn't know what to make of her gesture, but it felt like I wasn't given a choice. I looked down at that veiny age-spotted hand and then I took a hold of it. Her broad smile told me that I'd made the right decision. I noticed just then that this woman also had the smooth and plump lips of a younger woman as well. I had to wonder if that were another area of plastic surgery or if she were simply blessed.

"Look at *you* coming into our recovery center to stir things up! You're going to upset quite a few people, I hope you realize that," she grinned as she actually led the way toward the bar, keeping my hand in hers.

This lady had a lot of energy and she moved with such grace and elegance that I had to wonder if she had once been a model. She wasn't the slightest bit grandmotherly at all. As a matter of fact, she made me feel like I was escorting a queen or a princess into the bar.

"Now, you were so kind as to namelessly introduce yourself to all of us this morning at breakfast. I had to figure you out after that bold move, so I learned through the grapevine that you are Donner Michaels and it's very nice to meet you," she turned to me just inside the bar, taking both of my hands in hers, "My name is Piper Smith and it's very nice to make your acquaintance."

"Piper!" I repeated a little too abruptly.

She tilted her head, "You've heard that name already."

I shifted uncomfortably, looking down at my hands that were still held inside of her own. At this point, I really didn't know anything about her beyond what my prejudicial mind had already decided. As such, I felt I really had nothing to hide from her.

"Only in warning. A nice little lady from the third floor told me to watch out for Piper. I didn't know what it meant."

She expelled a throaty guffaw, then it seemed her entire body took part in the hearty laugh that followed. She even threw her head back as she released my hands. A moment later, she held her belly as she tried to gather her wits.

"I'm sorry," she shook her head as she finally settled down, "You see, it seems that there are many here who see me as something of a predator merely because... well, because I still focus a lot of attention on my appearance just like we all did in our younger years. I'm not the only one, however. Jeanette, Sarah, and Georgia are lovely women who haven't let go of themselves. But for some odd reason, those who are currently in relationships feel that I'm planning to lure their lovers away from them. But that just shows that they clearly don't know me at all. I'd never try to steal anyone's man. That would be horrible, hateful, and simply unladylike."

"Well that's good to know, Piper," I smiled, "I'd imagine you could probably lure a lot of those men away if you really tried. You're a lovely lady and it's good to know you're just as lovely on the inside."

"Why, thank you so much, sweetheart!" she leaned in and kissed me on the cheek, "You're not so bad yourself, Donner."

Truly, I do believe that if I were one of those older men back at the hotel, I'd be pursuing this very lady. It wasn't common to see women her age that could actually be classified as sexy and alluring. Again, I was quite proud of her and hoped that she ended up getting the pick of the litter for all her meticulous efforts.

I glanced over her shoulder and saw that there were four pool tables situated under four decorative stained-glass lights. Beyond those tables was a long bar with about a dozen empty barstools. On the right side of the room was a small video arcade consisting of four pinball machines and probably ten or so digital videogames. There were also the usual prize machines scattered throughout as well.

"I guess we get our choice of pool tables this early in the day," I said.

She had still been looking at me up to that point, so it took her a moment to comprehend what I'd said. She twisted around quickly and looked toward those tables.

"Oh yeah, the pool tables. Why don't you go grab us a couple of light beers while I select a nice table?" she asked.

"I'm not twenty-one!" I chuckled.

"And this isn't the United States!" she patted me on the shoulder, "Drinking age is eighteen here in Brazil, so enjoy it while you can."

I patted my pockets just then as I looked over toward the bar, "I don't have any money."

"And neither does anyone else. We're here on Khayyat's dime, kid. Everything is free. So stop delaying and treat your lovely date to a beer!" she urged.

I finally laughed. She was the first one here who truly seemed to view me as a peer and I liked that a lot. I didn't need any more grandparents in my life. I needed a friend who would joke around and toy with me like she was doing. I'd even venture to guess that she didn't have any children or grandchildren judging by the way she'd been talking to me. It was refreshing.

I made my way over to the bar where I only had to wait a few seconds before a middle-aged lady appeared from the doorway near the taps. She smiled at me as she quickly approached.

"What can I get you?" she asked.

"Can I get a light beer and a Cherry Coke?" I asked.

"Sure! Bottle or draft?"

I shrugged, not sure which was better. The broad-shouldered brunette leaned toward me.

"Is the beer for Piper?" she whispered.

I was startled by her question which caused me to pay a quick glance behind me. Piper was currently examining a cue stick, so she must not have heard our exchange.

"Yes," I replied.

"Draft then. And if she has more than two, make sure she eats something," she whispered.

"Okay," I wasn't able to hide the confusion as I arched an eyebrow.

"If you're seriously here to play billiards and have a good time, she needs to stay sober. And don't get me wrong – she often controls her drinking quite well. Just know that we've got plenty of pretzels and nuts. We even offer pizza by the slice," she whispered, "She's racking the balls already, so you'd better get over there."

That was when I realized that she'd already managed to pour the beer and the Cherry Coke without me noticing. I took both of the frosty glasses and then headed over to the pool table where Piper was patiently waiting. Again, this elderly woman happened to be posed like you'd imagine a twenty year-old model to be posing with her hip up against the pool table with a cue stick in her hand. I'd bet she seriously spent a lot of time in front of the camera back in her day.

"No beer for you?" she asked, taking the beverage that I handed to her.

"Tried it last year at a party and didn't really like it," I lied.

In truth, I just didn't understand why people liked to make themselves lose their inhibitions while at the same time getting dizzy in the process. If I wanted to get dizzy and have a good time, I'd go to the fair or an amusement park. She took a large drink from her glass and then set it down on one of the tall tables nearby. I took a quick sip of my cool beverage as well and then set my glass next to hers.

"Well, I'm the one who invited you, so you get to break," she said.

I went over to the wall rack and chose a stick that felt comfortable, then I made my way to the opposite end of the table. I scooted the cue ball onto the mark, then lined up my sight on it. I pulled back and then struck it hard, causing it to slam perfectly dead center into the front-most ball. The grouping of balls scattered nicely across that end of the table, but nothing dropped into the pockets.

"Nice break. You set me up on the seven," she said, moving around to the right side of the table.

She was right about the seven ball. It was a shot she couldn't miss. I watched from behind as she lined up her shot. That was the second time today that I noticed her unnaturally perfect curves. I honestly wasn't the type to objectify women in this manner and I certainly never looked upon my elders in such a way. But when a perfectly-shaped backside was bent over in front of a warm-blooded male, that warm-blooded male takes notice whether he intends to or not. It seriously made no sense to me however. Yeah, breast implants could understandably improve the size and shape of breasts of any age, but how does one maintain those curves in other areas such as this? That thought made me wonder just why it was that she was wasting her morning with me instead of the many prospects out there who were probably pining for this fine woman.

She knocked the cue ball perfectly into the seven, sinking it immediately. The cue ball bounced off the side, offering her no easy shots as far as I could tell.

"Looks like I'm solids and you're stripes," she said as she examined the table.

"Do you mind if I ask you a personal question?" I inserted.

"Two in the corner pocket," she said as she leaned down and lined up her shot, "Sure, ask away. I'm an open book, Donner."

Now she was leaned down across from me, knowingly offering me a view of her significant cleavage. Surely she knew what I could see considering the way she was dressed as well as the surgeries she'd undergone. I chose to respectfully look away and to focus my attention on the shot she was planning to take instead.

"Why did you choose to spend your morning inside a dark bar with the outcast of the 'Khayyat Nursing Home' rather than with your own peers?" I asked, "And I'm certainly not complaining. I'm grateful that someone was kind enough to reach out to the uncomfortable person who doesn't fit in."

"Outcast?" she laughed, taking the shot.

She hit the two-ball as intended, but the shot wasn't precise enough. That ball hit the edge of the corner pocket and then bounced over toward the other edge. I took that moment to examine the table for my first real shot. The balls were scattered about nicely, however the eight-ball was parked dangerously close to the far corner pocket where most of my prospects were.

"You are *certainly* not an outcast, Donner. Heck, you are the envy of us all. If there are haters in that building back there, it's because they're jealous of your youth. And those of us who aren't haters – well, we simply envy you for winning the ultimate lottery. I mean, look around you! We all hit the jackpot, but we're too old to really enjoy it like we would have in our younger years. Yeah, we're all healthy and our energy levels are wonderfully heightened, but that doesn't change appearances. But Donner Michaels though? That guy gets to enjoy this amazing paradise while he's still in his prime!"

I moved around the table to get a good shot on the eleven ball. I'd need to nick that ball on the left side if I intended to tap it into the side pocket.

"So, you aren't a hater. You want to live vicariously through me and to see how I viewed my current situation," I observed just before I took my shot.

To my surprise, I sunk the eleven ball but after the cue ball settled, it left me with no opportunities at all. I examined the table and found nothing of interest. I still had to consider the possibilities of inadvertently dropping the eight-ball with anything I hit.

"I want to know everything there is to know about the boy who should have died from the amoeba. You've been given a second chance and I wanted to be part of that second chance," she said, shrugging as she watched me.

I paused just then and looked over at her. She merely smiled beautifully at me in return.

"You really are a pleasant person to be around, Piper. Thank you sincerely for gracing me with your presence on a day when I was really feeling a little down," I said.

"Oh, sweetheart, now you are going to make me cry. I didn't even know you were depressed or I'd have chased you down sooner," she said, making her way quickly over toward me.

Before I knew it, I found myself wrapped in a surprisingly strong embrace. I held her tightly in return, realizing that I had really needed a good hug just then. We probably held this embrace for upwards of a full minute.

"Thank you again," I breathed.

She drew back and I could see that she truly did have tears in her eyes, "You're welcome, Donner. Just know that I'm going to be here for you anytime night or day."

She kissed me on the cheek, then patted me on the shoulder, "Still your turn."

SIX

We ended up playing four games of pool, only one of which I'd actually won. She was a pretty good player for as humble as she was. After the fourth game, she asked if I wanted to go for a stroll in the surf while she showed me around the neighborhood. I immediately agreed, having enjoyed her company thus far. So we returned the balls to the rack beneath the table. Then we returned the cue sticks, and then headed out into the sunny world outside of the Shipwreck.

I found myself shielding my eyes when we exited the bar. After an hour or so inside that dimly lit bar, the sun seemed far more intense now than it had been earlier. By the time I could comfortably see again without squinting, I noticed that the boardwalk and the beach were far more populated now. There were several beach umbrellas stabbed into the sandy beach at various locations. I could see those two men I'd stumbled upon back on the fourth floor riding those neon body-boards out in the surf. There was even a group of four women wading up to their knees in the water.

As we reached the small set of stairs that led from the boardwalk down to the sandy beach, Piper paused and grabbed the railing while she reached down to slip off her flip-flops. I followed suit.

"Would you care to take a lady's hand while we sink our toes into this sandy beach?" she said, offering me her left hand while she held her flip-flops in her right.

"I'd love to, your grace," I curtseyed as I shifted my shoes to my left hand and then took her hand into my right.

"Your grace?" she chuckled as we made our way down the three steps.

"What can I say? You carry yourself with such poise and elegance that one could only imagine you as a member of royalty. I feel like I'm escorting a princess onto the beach," I said.

We sunk our feet into the soft, warm sand. Walking now in the shifting sand was a little harder than up on the boardwalk.

"*Well*! Now aren't you the sweetheart. I swear, if you're trying to lasso this heart of mine, you're going about it in all the right ways, young man!"

"Good to know!" I laughed.

She seemed to truly require my presence as she held tightly to my hand. It wasn't long before we reached the firmer wet sand near the ocean's furthest reaches. Although we had better footing now, she kept hold of my hand, leading the way down to where the incoming surf could cool off our ankles and feet.

"So, tell me about the pre-Alzheimer's Piper," I said as we started in the direction of the hotel.

The cool surf came in and wonderfully soaked our lower calves, drawing a squeal out of piper.

"Whoa, that's a little colder than I had expected," she laughed as the surf receded, "Pre-Alzheimer's Piper? That's who I am today actually. Don't forget that these people you look at around here are just like they were before the disease could ravage them."

"I mean, you know, back home. Where are you from? What did you do for a living? Do you have a husband, children, grandchildren?" I asked.

"I knew what you meant. I was just hoping to avoid talking about me for as long as possible. I've really got nothing interesting to share," she looked over at me.

The cool surf snuck up on us again, but we were prepared this time for that chilly seawater as it drown our feet and ankles.

"I highly doubt that! Whatever city you hail from, I'm confident that there's a noticeable void in that place right now."

"How *old* are you, Donner?" she stopped abruptly and turned to me, "Did they use another experimental drug on you to make you look nineteen? Surely you're older than you look!"

"I'm seriously nineteen, Piper. I'd just turned nineteen two weeks before I contracted the brain-eating amoeba. I just graduated high school a few months ago. I'm nothing more than a shift supervisor at the Ponderosa Steakhouse in Akron, Ohio," I argued, "You seriously look mad. Do you really believe that I'm lying to you?"

I saw her shoulders relax just then as she held my gaze. Then she finally shook her head as she placed her hand on my cheek.

"I've been around a long time, Donner. I was once married right out of high school, but I ended up divorced a year later. I never married again, though I'd had many relationships over the years. But none were serious enough to warrant ever getting married again. And I think that's because common decency, respect, and romance isn't what it used to be back in my day. When I was a child, I fantasized about the man I'd marry and I held firmly to those things I believed a husband should bring to the relationship," she said, gazing upon me, "You, however, with the way you speak and the way you seem to build people up… well, you make me feel that there might still be hope for the upcoming generation. You're a beautiful young man, Donner Michaels."

"Thank you," I smiled, "And you're a beautiful young lady, so how about we continue our stroll and see how far this beach goes?"

She still gazed at me as she then breathed out something that I didn't quite understand. She then took my hand and started off toward our original destination.

"So, seriously, where are you from?" I asked, "I imagine you're from Ohio as well since Doctor Khayyat is operating out of the Cleveland Clinic."

"No, oddly enough I'm from Baltimore, Maryland. Doctor Khayyat and I dated back when he was going to school at Johns Hopkins. I had been a dancer at the night club he frequented. You should have seen me back in the day, Donner. I wasn't always old. Anyway, although the relationship didn't last, we'd stayed in touch all these years. Then, as the most unwanted gift anyone could get for their sixty-third birthday, I found out I was in the beginning stages of early-onset Alzheimer's. Needless to say, I called up my favorite neurosurgeon as soon as I could get to a phone. And before I knew it, I was on the next flight to Cleveland."

"Wow, saved by your ex! He must have still cared a lot for you," I said.

The cool surf continued to sneak up and soak our feet and ankles as we made our way further down the beach. I found it a little funny that we might as well have been the only two people in the whole world. Yeah, such a phrase could better be appreciated had we been a dating couple sharing a nice stroll on the beach. Instead, we were more along the lines of a couple of good friends separated by a few generations. She seemed to be as comfortable with me as I was with her.

"Yeah, he often checked in on me and we even gave the relationship a second try a few years later, but it just wasn't meant to be. I was never really meant to settle down which makes this sort of new life a little uncomfortable. Here, life is about as 'settled down' as it can get and we don't have a whole lot of control over our futures anymore," she said.

"But you're still not settled down with someone, right? You might be stuck living in that hotel back there, but you shouldn't be uncomfortable. Like you said earlier today – we hit the jackpot!" I encouraged her, "And if you decided to start dating, you could have your choice of any man in that building. I could only hope to be so lucky when I'm older."

"I haven't made a decision to actually stop dating. As a matter of fact, I'm truly not comfortable being alone. Who doesn't want someone to hold them every night? Who doesn't want to wake up to a tender kiss every morning?" she said, waving me off with those flip-flops in her other hand, "Ah, forget it. You're too young to understand. Just know that when you get older, it sucks to come home every day to an empty dark house. The loneliness is heartbreaking."

"No, please say it isn't so. And for the record, I'm not too young to understand loneliness. And I'm definitely not too young to wish I could be held every night or to be the one holding a lovely lady such as yourself," I sputtered just then as I fought to quickly clarify, "I-I mean no disrespect, Piper. Please know that I'm not suggesting sleeping with you! I'd never disrespect a fine lady like you in that way. I'm just... well, you're the definition of beauty, elegance, sweetness, kindness, and everything else a guy would want in a woman. I'm just explaining that I'm not a heartless idiot."

She stopped again midstride and turned to me, "I'd never suggest you're a heartless idiot. As a matter of fact, I believe you have a beautiful heart that seems to be much older than your years. I just hadn't realized that you understood loneliness like I do."

"Yes, I most certainly do. I'm actually even a little frightened to return to my room tonight. I've never spent a night out completely alone and without my friends or family. So, no, I'm not some wild and tough, independent teenager."

"Then why don't you come stay at my place on the second floor!" she said, squeezing my hand in hers.

"Wait... what?" I sputtered.

"You and I, Donner. We're the same and we want the same things," she suddenly laughed as a thought occurred to her, "Oh my god! I didn't mean it in the way that it probably sounded! I'm saying, in a purely platonic way, we could enjoy each other's company while we borrow the companionship we both need in order to survive in this new world."

I nodded the entire time she spoke, "You really wouldn't be uncomfortable knowing that there was a young guy you really don't know sleeping just a few feet away from you on your sofa?"

"I know you, Donner. I feel I know you more than you even realize. You'd truly consider it, though?" she smiled.

"You're the only person who I feel comfortable around. You're the only person I can talk to. And since you're obviously beautiful, that's just one of those added bonuses to such an arrangement," I grinned.

"You've called me beautiful or lovely far too many times today for me to disregard this any longer. Would you be upset if I took it upon myself to kiss you, Donner?" she asked.

"No! Of course not! I already-"

I had thought she had been referring to a kiss on the cheek like she'd done twice already. But when she cut off my words, it was because her plump lips were pressed against my own. She cupped the back of my head in her hand as she kissed me with a gentle sweetness that I hadn't ever experienced before. I merely followed her lead due to my inexperience. I cupped the back of her head in my hand as well as I felt my lips parting. This gentle and intimate kiss seemed to go on for several minutes before our lips parted and she rested her forehead against my own.

"That's how it is?" I breathed.

"Is it?" I felt her breath on my chin

"I think it is!" I whispered, "Is it wrong?"

"The only one to ask that question to would be yourself."

"It's so funny," I said, our foreheads still touching.

"Why?" she asked.

"It's funny because I honestly see nothing wrong with it. If anything, I feel a little unworthy."

"Then I'm glad you find it funny. And you are certainly more than worthy."

"So, then what now?" I asked.

"So… let me show you around the neighborhood just like we had originally planned when we left the bar."

"Sounds like a plan," I said.

SEVEN

We had to have strolled an entire mile through that cool ocean surf before we headed up the hot sands toward the boardwalk. We then stopped on the boardwalk stairs and did our best to brush the sand from our feet before donning our flip flops again. She took my hand as we started down the boardwalk toward the direction of the hotel. Along the way, we passed several restaurants, a variety of stores including a decently large book store, and even a beachfront bowling alley which also promised to offer billiards and a video arcade. We didn't go inside to confirm this. We did however stop to browse around inside a sunglasses store where we ultimately found ourselves some stylish sunglasses.

After that, we stopped by a little hot dog stand and had ourselves an early lunch right there on the boardwalk. We walked as we consumed our dogs.

"What are your plans should we be permitted to return to the US to continue our treatment?" I asked, licking the ketchup from my finger.

"If that were to happen, I'd have to believe we'd still be stuck inside some form of nursing facility. I doubt we'd be allowed to actually go home," she said, "So I sort of hope we stay here where it's more along the lines of a constant vacation."

I pondered this, taking a huge bite of my steaming hot dog. I hadn't really thought about that particular down side to being back in Ohio. This place was certainly far better than any Ohio nursing facility. I wondered just then what Piper's home life was like. She'd mentioned being a dancer once upon a time, which I understood was really just a more attractive title for a risqué sort of occupation. But surely Piper wasn't doing that sort of work in recent years.

"Were you retired back home?" I asked, "And let's imagine if we weren't stuck in a nursing home in Ohio. What if we were sent home and offered the chance to simply medicate ourselves? What would your plans be?"

She sighed, "Yes, I was retired. So, I'd probably go back to collecting on my retirement. I have no real family to speak of, so I could go back to Baltimore, Cleveland, or to Akron. Wherever the road leads me."

"Good," I muttered.

"Good? Are you saying you'd take this old lady back to meet your parents if something happened to permit such a thing?" she peered over at me as she finished off her hot dog.

"You just don't get it. I can only see you through my own eyes and no one else's. And as such, I simply don't see an old lady. I'm sorry if that's wrong or if you disagree. Yes, I guess if things progressed somehow between us, then I couldn't care less what other people thought."

"You really are a prize, Donner," she put her arm around me and pulled me close.

"Speaking of my parents. I'd like to go message them when we get back," I said, "What are your plans for this afternoon?"

"I'll probably go work out while you go message your parents. That usually takes me about an hour. After that, I typically like to relax in the hot tub for a while if you wanted to join me."

"Where's that?" I asked, wiping my mouth with the napkin and then tossing it into a nearby trashcan.

"Just follow the signs for the pool on the first floor."

EIGHT

I was glad to discover that the internet cable attached to my laptop was long enough to allow me to sit outside on my bedroom balcony. I'd sat down on the wicker chair while I enjoyed the salty tropical breeze. I opened that laptop, then I clicked that Text-Mail icon and selected both of my parents again.

"Hi Mom and Dad," I typed, "I was wondering if you could reach out to Doctor Khayyat for me and see if he has a timeline in mind for our return. Surely he must have an idea how long these things can take. And I was seriously wondering if they might want to send some high-ranking medical types down here to check these people out. My fellow cell-mates are all doing better than they've ever been prior, so it sort of bothers me that this isn't making national headlines. There should be reporters from all top news agencies hovering around down here. Anyway, I spent my morning with a very nice lady named Piper and I'm probably going to be hanging out with her this afternoon as well. She was another Alzheimer's patient of Khayyat's who is doing wonderfully. She's fun to be around and seems to really get me. And if you can believe it, she's quite attractive. Well anyway, we shot a few games of pool and she even beat me at three out of four games. I look forward to hearing from you. Love you lots! Donner."

After that, I closed my laptop and set it down on the small wicker end table next to me. I looked down at the beach below, happy to see that the majority of these residents had chosen to head out there today to enjoy the weather. I decided that it was time to start appreciating this place for the blessing that it really was. Even if I ended up being stuck here for a year, what did I have to complain about besides missing my family? This place was a literal tropical paradise and by Doctor Khayyat taking away the need for money, I would seriously want for nothing.

It warmed my heart as I watched those people socializing and enjoying themselves. These people most certainly had families back in the United States and I'd imagine some of those families were pretty huge given their ages. Yet they all somehow managed to put that all behind them and live for the moment. Maybe it was time I did the same.

"Donner, is that you over there?" a voice called from my left.

"Yeah Earl, it's me," I replied.

"Saw you out there with Piper on the beach this morning. Don't want to see you get hurt, bud. I'd recommend doing a little research before taking it any further, if you know what I mean."

I glanced over at that concrete wall that separated our balconies and I found myself shaking my head. It sounded to me like he wanted to share some unwelcome gossip. I had never expected to discover that my elders were the same sort of people that I went to high school with. I was actually disappointed with someone who was old enough to be my grandfather.

"I'll play the odds. I've found her to be the most pleasant company I've had in a long time, and that's including people from my old life as well. Thanks though."

"Good! That's great to hear. She's just been known to keep everyone at arm's length like she doesn't trust anyone. You'd never so much as even get a kiss from that Barbie Doll, much less anything else."

"Not even a simple kiss?" I found myself grinning, recalling those soft pink lips.

Counting the two kisses on the cheek, I'd already been the recipient of three kisses from that 'Barbie Doll'. That made me feel really special then.

"Nope, she's dated at least two guys here and they'll tell you that even after she's been drinking, you're not even getting to first base. She's nothing but a tease with a dream body."

"Well, that's good to know. If it's all the same, however, I'd just rather keep my relationships to myself. In her defense, maybe she'd been hurt before so she's overly cautious."

"If you're fine with 'cautious', then more power to ya'. At my age though? Heck, at *her* age? We just don't have time to play the good ol' 2-year courtship thing."

This guy was really starting to aggravate me. I grabbed my laptop and stood up.

"Listen, I've got to go. Nice talking with you," I said, wishing the sarcasm in my words was more evident.

I returned to my room and set the laptop back onto the charger. I then quickly changed into my swim trunks, grabbed a beach towel, and rushed out of the room.

NINE

It wasn't hard to locate the pool. Besides following the signs, I just needed to follow the scent of the chlorine. I opened the glass door and found myself faced with a pretty good-size swimming pool. There were three elderly men seated in the large hot tub to my immediate right. The only people occupying the pool at this time were an elderly black couple who were swimming side-by-side with pool noodles under their arms in the deep end.

I set my folded towel down onto one of the white plastic chairs, then I returned to the edge of the pool. That was the moment when I discovered the hotel's gym located just beyond that giant tinted window on the other side of the pool. There were five treadmills lined up near the glass, all facing away from the swimming pool. And even though she was currently running away from me, I could easily determine that it was Piper on that second treadmill wearing those tight black bicycle shorts and the black sports bra.

I dipped my toe into the water and found it to be a pleasantly cool temperature. I then leapt into the pool, kneeling down right away in order to submerge myself completely. I finally broke the surface and wiped my eyes.

"Amoeba Guy!" the Morgan Freeman look-alike smiled at me, "Are you sure that blob can't get out of you and back into the water?"

"You look around and see the sort of amazing ReMIND success stories around here and you think Doctor Khayyat might have missed a spot inside of me?" I asked.

"Just checkin' on your confidence levels, kid," he chuckled, "Name's Antonio."

"I'm Donner – nice to meet you, Antonio," I said, swimming over to shake his hand.

"This here is my wife Candace," he said, shaking my hand.

Candace wore her hair in a natural afro which looked nice on her. She reached out her hand and shook mine.

"Nice to meet you, Candace," I said, "A married couple that got Alzheimer's at the same time?"

"Oh no, we weren't married before we arrived here. We met here, fell in love, and the good Doctor Laekin married us. She's an ordained minister. Pentecostal apparently," Candace offered.

"That's awesome! Well congratulations and I'm glad that you two got more than just a second chance at life. You ended up with a second chance at love. Who could ask for anything more?"

"Amen, brother!" Antonio laughed, "I'm glad you got a second chance at life as well. Oh, and when you have a moment, there's a good burger joint down the way that you've *definitely* got to try."

"Do you have to greet everyone here with a recommendation for Burger Shack? Sounds like you own stock in the place," Candace splashed her husband.

"Hey, when I get a perfect double cheeseburger, I tell everyone!" he said, turning to me, "You've never had a better burger, I guarantee it!"

"I'll make sure to try it out. I, too, understand the value of a perfect burger. There are way too many variables involved that can ultimately mess up the final product! Cheese quality, bun size and freshness, crisp lettuce, quality condiments, fresh tomatoes, crisp pickles, and all the possibilities of the patty itself. You mess up just one of these things, and the perfection is lost!" I offered, getting a high five from Antonio even before I finished that last sentence.

"A match made in heaven," Candace shook her head while Antonio and I laughed.

"See, this man gets it!" Antonio pointed his thumb in my direction, "We're a rare breed, Donner."

After that, I grabbed a couple of foam noodles from the side of the pool and then proceeded to make myself a little seat in the water. One noodle cradled my knees and the other cradled my butt. I then casually paddled slowly around the pool, enjoying the cool water and the peace.

I couldn't gauge how much time had passed before Piper opened the glass door from the gym and discovered me in the pool. I waved over at her, curious just then as I realized for the first time that she actually had six-pack abs. How was that even possible for someone of her age? She waved and rushed over once she realized that it was me who had been waving to her from the pool.

"You came down here early to swim?" she asked, seating herself now at the edge of the pool.

I swam toward her where her legs dangled into the water. I had almost reached the edge when she slid herself into the water and tucked both of her hands behind my head. She then pulled me in for a quick kiss on the lips. This garnered some very audible gasps and echoing whispers from the direction of the hot tub.

"Perhaps the channel isn't of someone's liking," Piper whispered against my lips as she wrapped her legs around my waist.

I decided to test the growing relationship by gripping her around the hips and holding her to me. I could still read the smile in her eyes, so I assumed that the placement of my hands was acceptable.

"Perhaps someone is jealous of me," I whispered, leaning in and kissing those plump lips of hers.

"If my peripheral vision is to be trusted, I think there's at least two women in that hot tub. Maybe they're jealous of *me*," she leaned her head back, doing what it was that she did best.

As I'd already mentioned before, Piper had to have been a model at some point in her past. She knew all the right poses and this was clearly another one because as she leaned her head back and pulled away from me, it appeared that she was offering me her neck and then those enormous breasts that had already been fighting to break free from that small bikini top. I decided to play along as I drew her back to me and kissed her repeatedly down the front of her neck. She tilted her head to the side, offering me access to her collar bone. I kissed all along that collar bone until I reached the strap of her bikini top.

"They're leaving," her laugh echoing as she then gripped the back of my hair in her fist and pulled my lips to hers.

"Are we bad?" I asked between kisses.

"I should hope *so!*" she laughed again.

"Looks like the hot tub is all yours now if you want it!" Antonio hollered.

I turned to him and laughed. Both he and Candace had actually been watching in appreciation rather than judgement.

"Don't let them get to you," Candace offered.

"I was already catching it from my neighbor upstairs. It's why I came down here early," I said, realizing just then that both of my hands were firmly planted on Piper's butt while I held her to me.

Both of her legs were still clamped tightly around me, clearly claiming me as her own.

"Someone was harassing you because of me?" Piper asked.

"Yeah, but I didn't want to hear it, so I just left."

"See, nothing I do will ever be right in these people's eyes," she groaned, "First, these women think I might steal away their lovers. Then when it's clear that I'm interested in someone *besides* their men, that's wrong as well."

"That's why we need to seal ourselves inside our own little bubble. I don't care what anyone thinks. I like spending time with Piper," I argued, "She's interesting and makes me happy."

"Do you really not care?" she asked, looking at me with pleading eyes.

"I seriously one-hundred percent don't care whatsoever. I'm in a whole new world and now this new world involves unusual experiences that I'd have never imagined before. I'll take it!" I said.

And for the next minute or so, I got to experience one of those curiously intimate and almost sexual kisses from Piper. I wasn't even sure how she could take a kiss and make it so sensual, but she did.

TEN

We had spent about a half hour in the hot tub while I shared all the details of my life. I hadn't intended on this, but she kept asking and I kept sharing. By the time we were done, she had come to the conclusion that my ongoing sanity would be dependent upon a collection of mystery novels. When I asked her where such a thought came from, she proceeded to take apart the details of my entire life like Sherlock Holmes would have done back in the day.

"It's simple, actually. Every single time that you've found yourself in a rough spot or simply when you've been hurt or confused, you then started to tell me about 'this one book I read'. If you look back, I'm sure you'll notice that you were reading these novels as a result of emotional turmoil, confusion, or distress. You obviously read to decompress. So, if I'm going to pursue an ongoing relationship with you, then I want to make sure you have some enjoyable novels around to keep that even keel. We're going book shopping, Donner!"

I laughed, "So you mean to tell me that you're the one pursuing me? And on top of it all, you're going to set up all the necessary chess pieces in order to make sure that there's ultimately a check-mate?"

She looked at me for a moment, then simply replied "Yes!"

"And you're blatantly honest?" I burst.

She shrugged, then nodded, "Yes! Let's go to the bookstore!"

And just like that, the two of us draped our towels over us and then proceeded half-naked and barefoot out of the 'hotel' and down the boardwalk toward that bookstore we had passed by earlier.

"So, fill me in. Do you go for those massive thousand-page sagas or are you more of a fan of the two hundred page thrillers? I only ask because I usually only read Nicholas Sparks, Mitch Albom, or Charles Martin who typically lean toward the two hundred page novels."

"I'm more in between the two. I like a good thriller or mystery that often ends up in the grocery store as a mass-market paperback. Those are oftentimes around three-fifty or four hundred pages, give or take," I replied.

"Okay, and when you read… tell me a little about this," she insisted.

"Why do I feel that I'm being interrogated?" I chuckled, gesturing toward the bookstore, "Looks like we're here."

"I just wanted to get an idea. Do you read in bed until you fall asleep? That's me, by the way. Do you read after dinner on the couch? Do you read on the beach? What's your preference? I want to place these chess pieces in all the right places."

I laughed and turned to her, "You're really having fun with this, aren't you?"

"I want Donner!"

"You have me! I'm going nowhere!" I placed a hand on her cheek.

"Yeah? What happens when Doctor Khayyat cures an eighteen year old cheerleader of a brain-eating amoeba? What happens when this little doll shows up in a suite on the fourth floor?"

"You've really thought this out and it goes to show just how smart you truly are. You've examined the entire battlefield and I can appreciate that. But what you fail to realize is that I've only got eyes for you, Piper. Nothing on Earth is going to change that," I said, touching her youthfully plump lips with the tip of my finger, "And I love to read at times like this when we've had a nice day together and we need a moment to simply relax and unwind. I'd love to just lie on a towel on the beach and tear into a novel."

"You never cease to amaze me, Donner. And I really hope that you truly only have eyes for me."

"Hey, it's already settled that I'm sleeping on your sofa tonight. You're stuck with me! That hasn't changed."

"Actually, yes it has, Donner."

"What?"

"My sofa isn't the place for you. You're sleeping in my arms tonight. This isn't up for debate," she argued.

I merely stared at her in awe.

ELEVEN

I had found myself six paperback novels that really intrigued me. Piper even found two that interested her as well. We left that store and then headed straight out there onto the hot sand of the beach. The choice to head out to the beach was all due to my statement that I wanted to lie on a towel on the beach and read a good novel.

Thankfully, the sun was hiding behind random clouds now, so lying on the beach without an umbrella wasn't as painful as it could have been. We both tossed our towels down onto the sand and then proceeded to lie face-down while we sifted through our bags. I settled on a Joseph Finder thriller while Piper dug into the most recent Nicholas Sparks.

While it had been a quaint and comfortable way to spend an afternoon, the two of us were bored with it after a half an hour. While I was most certainly engrossed in the novel, I couldn't deny the restlessness in my mind. After all, I had just lost my family and friends. I had also just discovered Piper and everything else that this wonderful woman entailed. Piper was amazing and awesome, yet she was more than three times my age! And no, this didn't bother me one bit, but I could appreciate how it would bother the rest of the world, my parents included. And I also had to deal with the fact that I truly believed now that this banishment from the US was actually forever. I'd seen enough acceptance and complacency from those around me to confidently make this assessment.

We saw the restlessness in each other and decided to leave those novels with our towels and then head down into the cool surf. I took Piper's hand and then ran into the water until the Atlantic was all the way up to my knees. I then tugged Piper to me and asked her the one question that had recently demanded my attention.

"Are you real, Piper? Just say it with your own lips. Speak it and I'll believe it."

"Real? Are you finally understanding what I meant when I demanded your real age? You're wondering too! Isn't it crazy?" she asked.

I stepped back, then looked down at her belly. I traced those rigid lines with my pointer finger. Sure, there were those subtle and leathery crinkles that always came with age, but I could still see the musculature of the six-pack.

"You didn't answer my question. I've kissed those lips, so I trust them. Tell me you're real."

"Donner, my name is Piper Smith and I'm one hundred percent real. If there's a deception around us, which I believe might actually be a possibility, I'm certainly not part of it."

"That's enough for me, then," I knelt down into the cool water and I kissed her belly just above her navel.

I needed to feel that no-so-perfect skin against my lips. I kissed that belly button, then I began tracing the lines of her abdominal muscles with my kisses.

"No," she pleaded as she clutched my head to her stomach, "I can't take that sort of teasing unless it's going to progress all the way and we both know it's certainly not at this time."

I gently kissed my way up her body and then to her lips. She reached up and quite forcefully grasped two fistfuls of my hair, fighting to keep my lips against her own. Even if I had wanted to escape, I couldn't for fear of losing my hair. If only Earl could see us now.

TWELVE

I had returned to my room only intending to take a shower, grab some clothing, and then make my way back to Piper's room. But the first thing I noticed upon my arrival was my chirping laptop. I rushed over to the sofa and quickly opened up the computer to discover that I had two messages. One of those messages was from my parents and the other was from my brother Brett. I opened the one from my parents first.

"Donner! It's always so good to hear from you. We're so glad to hear that you're making friends there and please say hello to Piper from us. We've been bugging Dr. Khayyat nonstop so believe us when we say we're trying to get answers. For now, it's honestly looking like a year or so, so please try to make yourself comfortable for now. If you go on thinking that it's only a weeklong stay, you might just shrug it off not really settle in like you probably should. Don't do that. Think of it as a yearlong stay so you won't be disappointed. Make friends. Have some fun. Enjoy that extended beach vacation for what it really is. And don't have so much fun down there that you end up forgetting about us in Ohio. We want to know all about your adventures down there in South America! Oh, and Aunt Nancy is actually dating again, if you can believe that. The guy is ten years younger, though! Seems odd, but maybe love doesn't ask for resumes first. She's happy though and her kids don't mind. Hey, we probably talked too long and really gotta go!

We love you more than you'll ever know! Please message us soon! Love, Mom and Dad"

I sighed, worried that they might have been right. Maybe this was truly going to be my semi-permanent residence for an extended period of time. Maybe I needed to plan for that and make the best of it. I pondered this as well as Aunt Nancy's similar relationship for a moment, then I glanced down at the icon for Brett's message. I then clicked that unread message from my brother.

"Donner bro! I love you. You know this. Hey, make the best of it and do absolutely everything with no regard for the consequences. It doesn't matter because it's freaking paradise there, dude! Seriously though, I need to drop some brutal honesty on you! Stop asking about when you'll ever get to come back to the States because it ain't happening. Ask everyone there! There are always delays or excuses, but in the end, it's scientifically impossible for you to ever return. It will <u>never</u> happen even if Christ returned today. And please know my heart, bro – I'm not trying to hurt you. I want you to enjoy what you've been given! Mom and Dad have all the scripts so they know what to say to your concerns. But I don't have those scripts, so I'm here to tell you like it is. You and your friends can't return to the US because it's simply impossible. The only people you'll ever physically interact with again are those who have also taken part in the same ReMIND experiment. That's good though because they're real. You're real, they're real, and the rest... well, reply to me if you want further details dude. I want to hear what you think first. Have fun, though! Miss you!"

I read his message three times. This was alarming. I knew my little brother well enough to accept that he would probably be the only one to give it to me straight. Sure, we joked around a lot and even got into some pretty intense fights, but neither of us would ever hurt each other with a gag. Neither of us were fans of the supposedly hilarious practical jokes that people often pulled on each other.

He had gone so far as to say that I couldn't return home even if Christ returned today. That was a frightening statement because we both had a lot of respect for our Savior and nothing was beyond Jesus' control. However, Brett pretty much said that this situation that I found myself in actually was.

I then pondered the many options I had at my own disposal. I could just as easily leave this place. There were no gates or barbed-wire fences. Sure, I didn't currently have any money, but I could find a way to get some. I could sell my surfboard. I could sell anything that I chose to take from any of these stores. Then I could take a cab to the airport and catch a flight home. Why was Brett so absolutely certain that I couldn't ever return even not knowing what I had available to me here?

I decided to ask him. I clicked his name, then started typing.

"Brett, it's great to hear from you, however now I'm a little concerned. Why are you so confident that I can never return home again? And you mentioned that I and the others here in the nursing home are real. Does that mean that some of these people aren't? Both Piper and I had already been suspicious of each other, so I doubt you can say anything that would shock us. How are Mom and Dad holding up – for real? And please answer this question: was my agreement to go along with this ReMIND experiment treated as though I had died back home? Basically, was my departure to South America seen as though I'd died? I look forward to hearing back from you. Please take care of the chores around the house. Mom and Dad are getting old and need some help. Love you, bro."

I sent that off, then thought about contacting my parents. I stopped myself before I could tap their names on the screen. Although Dad had answered my question to prove to me it was really him, Brett had said something about scripts. Until I learned more, I thought it best not to contact them.

My heart jumped just then as someone knocked on the door. I was feeling quite paranoid all of a sudden, so this set my heart racing.

"Yes?" I hollered as I set my laptop down onto the table.

"Donner? It's Piper," she hollered back.

I rushed to the door and opened it. I inadvertently gasped when I discovered her standing there in a satiny plum dress. I gaped at her like any uncivilized Neanderthal would for an extended moment, then I stepped back and invited her in.

"You're not showered or dressed," she looked at me in confusion as she seemed to glide into the room.

"You look lovely and regal as always," I said, finding a smile returning to my stunned face, "And I might have been underdressed anyway had I actually *been* ready."

She turned to me as I closed the door, "So then tell me please - why would you leave a lady waiting?"

"I… uh…"

She rushed to me and pulled me into her arms, "I'm teasing, Donner! Now go take a shower quick shower and get dressed so we can go out to dinner!"

THIRTEEN

After merely a five-minute shower, I shaved and then put on one of my nicer suits. Then I came out of the bathroom to find Piper lying down on my bed facing away from me and sound asleep. I chuckled, listening to those snores as I eased my way onto the bed behind her. Then I lay on my side up against her and kissed her on the cheek from behind, intending to gently wake her. She mumbled something, then started to snore again. I chuckled, realizing just then that she was really sound asleep. Six o'clock might have been a little early to go to bed, but then again, this was a nursing home. I sat up just then, loosened my tie, then took it off and tossed it onto the sofa. I slid my pillow directly behind her head and then I lie down, spooning her from behind. I draped my arm over her at the waist and pulled myself as close to her as I could get.

And a moment later, I found that the dream world had required my presence as well.

FOURTEEN

At some point in the night, I heard my mother's annoying blue parakeet. I don't recall how many times it tweeted before I finally woke up feeling a little aggravated. The first thing I noticed in the dark room was that someone was currently seated on the sofa leaning over my laptop. The light from the laptop screen highlighted the familiar features of Piper. I lay my head back down onto the pillow as I watched that beautiful lady who was still wearing that elegant dress.

Then I suddenly sat up as the tweets of that blue parakeet immediately came to mind. That chirping I'd heard was actually the message alert from my laptop! And Piper was currently seated on the sofa looking down at my laptop!

I switched on the lamp, startling Piper who now had a very guilty expression on her face.

"I… well, it kept chirping, so I meant to shut off the audible alerts," she stood up quickly, "It's only nine-thirty if you still wanted to go out for dinner, sweetheart. The local beachfront restaurants stay open until eleven and the bars don't close until one."

"Did my brother reply to my message?" I asked, realizing that it really didn't matter if she'd read it.

"Umm… yeah. You mean Brett?" she still looked very worried as she approached, "Sorry I fell asleep, baby, but it sure was nice to wake up in your arms."

She caressed my cheek in her hand. I gave her a quick kiss on the lips just to reassure her.

"Listen, Piper. I don't care if you read the message. I would have shared it with you anyway. I just... please tell me if I really want to read it or not."

She was shaking her head as the tears started welling up in her eyes, "I really don't quite understand it and I'm not real sure I *want* to understand it."

"Should I read it?" I asked.

"I think you should wait until tomorrow. Let's share a night where your smile and your innocence are still as sincere and real as I want them to be," she asked, drawing me to her in an embrace, "Please, just one night of sweet innocence?"

I allowed myself to be held, resting my head on her shoulder, "So, what do you want to do?"

"Well, we can get into proper pajamas and go back to bed, or you can at least take off your jacket and shirt and we'll just go back to bed as we're dressed. Or if you're hungry, we can still do dinner."

"I'm afraid to even leave my room right now, so if it's all the same to you, I think I'd like to just lie in your arms. I was drowning in a raging sea of paranoia even before my brother replied."

She kissed my forehead and whispered a promise to hold me all night. And just like that, I took off my jacket and my shirt and then crawled back into bed. The door suddenly opened in that instant, surprising us both. I was about to leap from the bed when Laekin walked in with two syringes.

"No! What's this?" my paranoia demanded as I sat up in bed.

"This is our nightly meds, Donner," Piper said, appearing very concerned as she looked over at me.

"Well, you look awfully nice tonight, Piper!" Laekin said, quickly inserting the needle into her forearm and pressing down on the plunger, "A little overdressed for bed though."

She quickly stuck a bandage to Piper's forearm, then she tore open another bandage with her teeth. Laekin's efficiency was smooth and precise.

"Donner and I are going to Cinderella's Ball tonight in our dreams, so it's best to dress the part," Piper offered as an explanation.

"Well, then I think Donner might be a bit underdressed then," she said, glancing at my bare chest as she quickly jabbed the needle into my arm.

"Piper was in the process of tearing off all my clothes when you barged in and ruined the moment," I snickered.

Piper gasped, placing her hand over her mouth before she burst out laughing. Laekin merely looked at the two of us wide-eyed.

"Well, then I guess I should leave the two of you for now. Perhaps 'have fun' would be the most appropriate good-bye!" Laekin chuckled as she made for a quick departure.

"How dare you embarrass me like that!" Piper laughed, slapping me on the shoulder, "Imagine what all she's visualizing in that pretty little head of hers right now!"

"That's why I did it. That was a pretty rude interruption, so I wanted to make her as uncomfortable as I could," I explained.

Piper was still chuckling as she drew the covers up. She then patted the bed beside her, offering me to lie down on the pillow next to her. I lie down, then she reached over and switched off the light. I was lying down on my back as she cuddled up next to me, tucking one arm beneath me and then resting her hand on my stomach.

"Well, then I'm glad you did made her uncomfortable," she said, gently gliding those fingers across my chest and my belly, "Tell me what you want, Donner."

"This," I said, turning to face her and kissing her gently on the lips, "I want this and I want it every day and every night."

"Then that's what you'll have," she reached up and raked her fingers through my hair.

"Thank you for being so sweet, lovely, and understanding," I whispered.

She nuzzled her face close to mine, then drew her leg up over my own. She then kissed me sweetly on the lips while holding me in both of her arms.

"Go to sleep, sweetheart," she breathed, "I've got you."

FIFTEEN

I woke up right around the same time that the sun was peeking out above the ocean and dousing my room with its orange hues. I'd guess that it was somewhere between five-thirty and six o'clock. I had been lying on my back with Piper asleep on my chest. Her entire upper body was lying on me and one of her legs was draped across my own. I cautiously drew the blanket back, intending to slip out from underneath her, but that was when I discovered that she was naked save for a pair of lacy red panties. I had to admit that I'd wondered at one point last night just how uncomfortable that tight dress might have been. Her breasts alone had been straining against the seams of that dress. At some point during the night, she must have slipped out of it.

I drew the covers over the two of us again, realizing that she would probably need those sheets to protect her modesty once she woke up. She lifted her head just then, appearing to quickly assess where she currently was, then a moment later, she rested her head on my chest again.

"Any regrets yet?" Piper asked, lifting her head again and then resting her chin on my chest so she could look up at me.

"Certainly not!" I sputtered with a laugh, "To wake up with a beautiful naked woman in my arms? Well, that's the American dream!"

She laughed, "Yet you're not doing the sort of things you should be doing when you're presented with all these opportunities."

"Oh, that doesn't mean I don't want to. I'm a warm-blooded American male! I couldn't even imagine how it'll be when the time comes," I sighed, "I'd probably lose my mind."

"So, you're talking about it like it's definitely going to happen, but just not yet. Now, I hate to break it to you Donner, because I understand that you're a decent, tender, and loving man. But please realize that you wouldn't be deflowering me."

I laughed heartily at that. Her smirk told me that she was still waiting for an explanation. I now wondered if she had felt rejected by me all night long. I realized in that moment that her delicate fingertips had traced dangerously low a few times when she was tickling my belly and chest last night. In hindsight, perhaps that had been very intentional.

"There's a couple things actually. First… well, I guess you should know that you'd be deflowering *me*. I've never…"

"No, really?" she interrupted, leaning up on her arms.

This view was killing me now as her swollen breasts hung low and heavy against my belly.

"Yes, really. And, well I sort of want it to mean something. I believe it should be… you know, *forever.* It's precious I guess, so it's something that I believe is a bond between two people for the rest of their lives. And yeah, I'm confident that I could make that kind of commitment to you, but… but you'd only been married once for a short while and it doesn't seem like something you'd ever want to do again. And I get that. You've got a lifetime of-"

She rose up on those arms and scooted up so that she could plant her lips on mine. She kissed me deeply, raking her hand through my hair as she drew back.

"You value me more than most of the men I've ever been with, and yet you're technically just a kid in the grand scheme of life. You treat me like royalty or like something that should be treasured. So yes, I've lived a long life with a bunch of throw-away relationships. And maybe it's because I saw myself through their eyes. Maybe it's because I didn't value myself as much as I should have. But now I'm starting to see myself through *your* eyes and I really like what I see. I like the Piper that you see and that person really likes… *loves* you. You see, I don't need any more throw-away relationships. According to your brother, we're here forever, so all you need to do is say it, Donner. Say what it is that you're implying."

"He reiterated it again? We're really never going home again?" I breathed.

She sighed, deflated as she held my gaze. I continued to look at her in worry.

"Never. This is our home until the day we die which sadly, your brother has a date for that apparently," she said, gazing upon me with those pleading eyes.

"Brett knows when we're going to die? I'm confused," I sputtered.

"We can discuss that later. We're talking about the other stuff now. The other more important stuff," she said, "Focus, Donner."

"Oh…" I held her gaze, then looked down at those full pink lips, "Well, maybe I'm a bit naïve and one could argue that I might not know a whole lot about love, but I think I love you, Piper. I hope that doesn't scare you and if it does, I can't really apologize for it. It's just what it is. I want to spend all day today with you. I want to spend tonight with you as well. Then I want to spend all day tomorrow with you. I don't care if you always beat me at pool or if you destroy me at bowling. I do want to go check out that bowling alley soon, by the way. I don't care if we simply sit on the beach and read some novels together. I just enjoy spending time with you and talking and laughing. So, well I guess I'm saying that I love you and I'm willing to make that dedication to you for the rest of my life. I wonder if you might feel the same."

"I do," she started crying as she kissed me three times in a row, "Yes, Donner. I do love you and I'm willing to dedicate myself to you and you alone for the rest of our lives. So, if your valiant and chivalrous heart requires an actual marriage in order to enjoy the succulent desserts we both have to offer, then I'd suggest we meet with Laekin as soon as possible."

I chuckled, "Wow! I like your choice of words. You don't pull any punches."

"So you agree then?" she cocked an eyebrow.

I couldn't help but to smile as I held onto those teary eyes. She truly was beautiful and amazing in every way.

"Definitely, but first I should probably read my brother's message," I said.

"Yeah, I suppose that's probably best," she said with a sigh, "Why don't you get me my dress off the floor, then I'll get dressed and go to my room to wash up and make myself beautiful for you?"

"You're already beautiful," I kissed her, "So that part is already handled."

"You're too much, Donner!" she chuckled, rolling off of me as she wrapped herself in the bedsheet.

I got up from the bed and located that silky plum dress at the foot of the bed. I tossed it to her, which she caught as she rolled to the side of the bed. She remained wrapped in the bedsheet as she slowly made her way to the bathroom.

"So, what are the clothing plans for today?" I asked, "Because don't forget that I almost wore shorts and a polo while you were planning on that delicious dress. Are we dressing up or not?"

"If today is going to be the best day of our entire lives, which I firmly believe it will be, then let's keep it casual," she hollered back from the bathroom, "After all, how long are we going to spend in that clothing today anyway?"

SIXTEEN

After she got dressed, she excused herself from my suite. I spent a few minutes in the bathroom washing up, brushing my teeth, and then getting dressed in another pair of cargo shorts and a casual untucked blue button-up. I then made my way over to the sofa where the laptop still waited for me on the coffee table.

I hit the spacebar to bring the computer out of its sleep mode. There before me was Brett's message which had never been closed out. I leaned forward and read what it said.

"Well, Donner, I talked with your friends David and Bogey about all of this and together we ultimately decided two things. The one most important thing was that I was wrong for wanting to give you every single bit of truth. I had simply thought that was something that I'd want to know if I were in your position. But they helped me to realize that since you have no control whatsoever either way, then my idea could only serve to hurt you. Do you remember that time when we went to the Ohio State Fair and we went into that thing that looked like a windowless shrunken Winnebago? We sat down in that dark thing and strapped ourselves into those padded chairs and then suddenly the weird thing turned on. The entire inside was made up of video monitors, so it suddenly looked like we were at an amusement park. We were suddenly moving up the first hill of an old wooden rollercoaster and it felt so real even as the entire vehicle shuddered. Then suddenly we were shooting downhill and racing along the twisting track and it felt so real due to the gravitational effects! At the end of that rollercoaster, we suddenly found ourselves in the cockpit of a fighter jet. I think there were a couple other vehicles we found ourselves in by the time that thing was done,

"But man, that felt so real to us while it was going on! It wasn't until we got out of that Winnebago and watched that ride from the outside that we finally deflated. We were saddened to see all the hydraulics beneath that machine causing the whole unit to angle upward, then jar side to side. Now please don't get me wrong. You aren't in one of those illusionary machines like that. I'm just using that as an example of how we both had a great experience, and then it was snatched away when we learned about those behind-the-scenes details that we never needed to know. This is why I'm going in a different direction now. But as your brother, there are things I need to share with you. Yes, I already explained that you and all those other patients are completely real. You all can even have conversations via Text-mail with those of us you left behind. In truth, that's the biggest draw of Doctor Khayyat's ReMIND surgeries. We get to have ongoing contact with those who have had incurable neurological diseases and this sort of relationship can go on for years. *Ten* years as a matter of fact,

"Now here's something important that you need to know. This program you are part of is only approved and funded for ten years. That's it, bro! If they don't get approval for a continuation or if they don't get the funding they need, the program gets shut down. That's something I will not keep from you. Yes, you are never returning here to the US. Yes, you are stuck in that awesome paradise until the day you die. You and Piper – you two need to make the best of every moment you have because rest assured, you've only got ten years. And let's say they get the continuation they need and let's just say they get the funding. That's another ten years. It irritates me thoroughly that your lives are permanently at the hands of others and you're going to be given these ongoing blessings in ten-year increments,

"So that's what I came here to tell you. None of you can die unless the program gets shut down due to lack of funding or interest. There's going to be no cancer or heart attacks. Heck, there's going to be no more aging either. What you see is what you get and it will remain that way until you die due to lack of funding. I'm going to be an advocate for you guys starting today. I'm going to seek out the funding. I'm going to fight for you. Until that day comes, though, make the best of it. Go swimming in the ocean every single day, bro! And if Piper is the one, then go for it dude! If the food is amazing, then overindulge! Just know that through it all, there's a guy back home who is fighting for ten more years. As long as I live, I'm not going to stop,

"Oh, and when curiosity beckons and requires you to ask me those deep hidden questions, just know that I won't answer them. I'm your brother and I want you to enjoy every minute you have! Love ya!"

I stared at the screen for a moment, then I shook my head. Although he wanted me to be happy, he also subtly hinted that this might all be an illusion. At the same time, however, he wanted me to know that the important people around me were real. And he knew about Piper which meant that he talked to Mom and Dad.

Then I remembered that Piper had also read this message. I wondered just then if that had a role in her sudden change of heart. Whether or not it influenced her really didn't matter. Clearly she believed in all that my brother had said. She believed that our days were numbered, but that we'd also been guaranteed at least ten years. For me at my age, that wasn't such a big deal. But at Piper's age, it was probably a big deal to be given the promise of at least ten more years. That promise warmed my heart, recalling that she'd just said yes. She had promised those ten guaranteed years to me and here I was still sitting alone on the sofa in my bedroom.

I slammed that laptop shut, then leapt from the sofa and rushed to the door. I had a bride waiting for me!

SEVENTEEN

After a hearty breakfast of pancakes, sausage links, and orange juice, we made for a hasty trip to Doctor Laekin's office. Thankfully she was there, so we took a moment to explain our situation and merely asked for her blessing. She obviously had several questions to ask us in response, probably in an effort to gauge our overall understanding of such a lifelong commitment. And in the end, about fifteen or twenty minutes after we'd arrived there in her office, Donner and Piper were wed.

Now, one would probably expect to hear that we'd left that office in a mad dash and rushed upstairs to tear each other's clothing off, but I'm proud to say that such wasn't ever the real motivation or even the ultimate reason that we'd made those unbreakable vows. We truly did love each other and we actually wanted to spend time together. The rest was just a bonus that we would get to take advantage of when those opportunities naturally arose.

So, when we left Laekin's office, Piper took my hand in hers and then politely asked me if I wanted to get my derriere handed to me at the bowling alley. That was the moment that I knew for certain that I'd made the right decision in marrying this lovely woman. Even while she had been lying naked on top of me earlier, she had actually heard those words I'd spoken.

"I've bowled a two-twenty game before," I tilted my head in pride while we made our way out of the hotel and onto the boardwalk.

"Oh, I'm so sorry. Don't let that get you down, though," she said, putting her arm around me and drawing me close, "We all have our bad days."

I looked over at her, unsure if she had misunderstood. Her smirk told me she hadn't.

EIGHTEEN

It wasn't even time for lunch yet and here I was back in bed, our clothing scattered on the floor, while I still made an attempt to catch my breath. Piper was lying on top of me while her head rested on my shoulder. I could feel her breath against my neck as she also struggled to calm her racing heart. Both of my hands still held onto her nice bottom.

"I don't ever need to leave this bed again for the rest of my life," I breathed.

"And yet those were just two of the many ways!" she chuckled, "We've got so many more options and methods to explore."

"Just give me a moment," I pleaded, reaching up and holding the back of her head to me, "That took a lot out of me."

"Literally," she laughed.

We lie there in silence for a few more minutes before she finally spoke.

"What if this is all an illusion?" she asked, "Yeah, you and I are real. Antonio and Candace are real. The guy beating on the wall and demanding we keep it down is real."

"Earl," I breathed.

"Yeah, Earl is real," she placed her hands onto the mattress at each side of my head and then leaned up, "So let's just assume that all these people are real, but everything else isn't. Heck, we're probably not even in South America. What if that is the state of the world we're living in? Real people residing in a fake world."

"That's *exactly* what I believe this is. In such a place, I suppose one could be upset by the deception. But if the people are real, then what you and I have is real. There could be no denial in that. I don't care if this room is real or if that ocean is real. It all feels real to me and I appreciate that. But if you and your words and your heart weren't real, then I think I would certainly be hurt. But I'm confident that you're real and that's a good thing."

"And I believe you're real as well," she chuckled, kissing me.

"So I guess that means we're back to the only thing that matters in a world that might be an illusion - you and me. And I don't know about you, but I think I'm ready," I said.

She grinned, then grabbed me in both arms and rolled us over together as one entity. Now, apparently, it was my turn to be on top.

-NINE AND A HALF YEARS LATER-

Khayyat ReMIND Neurological Foundation

(Secure Underground Facility)

Brett had finally secured the funding necessary for another ten years of research. After donating those funds, he got to have his one wish granted. For years now, he had been wanting to see his brother, physically, one last time. That was why, today, he was being led down the stairs to a hidden facility beneath the Khayyat ReMIND Neurological Foundation on West Market Street.

His guide, a burly black security guard with a shaved head, entered a multiple-digit code into the keypad next to the sturdy metal door. Brett looked past the guard to see not only that bold black acronym, but also its meaning printed on the gray door. He'd always wondered if Donner ever discovered what ReMIND had stood for. There it was emblazoned on the door, however: **Re**animation – **M**ortally **I**mpeding **N**eurological **D**eterioration.

Mortally… that was probably the most important word on that door. That was the word that would have caused Donner to question things. Everyone knew what it meant to be mortally wounded or mortally injured. And Donner was smart. That was the reason Brett never shared the meaning of the acronym.

The guard opened the door and invited Brett to lead the way into the dimly lit room. At first, he thought the guard had brought him to the wrong place because it seemed that he was now inside an overly air-conditioned computer lab instead of a hospital or medical lab.

"What's his name again?" the guard asked in a deep voice as the door closed behind them.

"Donner," Brett said, "Donner Michaels."

The giant equipment inside the room hummed with that familiar sound of electronic life while some unknown processors and fans could be heard buzzing away at the other side of the room. The temperature in the room had to be much lower than sixty degrees.

The security guard led the way to the far side of the room where Brett had noticed probably a hundred or more small square aquariums tucked away into those many shelved cubbies spanning from the floor to the ceiling. Hoses, wires, and pipes made that entire wall look like a wild and unorganized mess. Yet, as Brett got closer, he could see that these glass aquariums were actually cylindrical in nature, each glass unit just a little larger than a coffee can in size and shape.

He also noticed that instead of clear water inside those jars, it was a greenish-yellow fluid surrounding something fleshy. That was when Brett stopped and caught his breath. Sure, he'd already known that his brother only existed in partial form anymore, but he'd never really thought about how small of a portion was required in order to maintain his ongoing existence.

The security guard examined several of those jars, each of which was firmly embedded into its own little pocket of the wall. He passed by about a dozen before he turned and pointed his finger at the jar about waist-high. Brett released the breath he'd been holding, then he took a few steps toward the jar in question. When he finally approached, the guard politely stepped aside to give him some privacy.

Brett knelt down and saw his brother's name imprinted on a decal at the top of the frightening jar. Inside the little glass vat, in that greenish-yellow fluid, he could see his brother's brain with electrodes and wires attached throughout its entirety. At the bottom of the jar, there was an odd black mechanical device about the size of his fist attached to the brain stem. This too had some wires leading from the device and out of the top of the jar. In all, there appeared to be a thick bundle of twenty or thirty wires that met together at the top and then ran into the wide metal pipe that spanned from the floor to the ceiling.

"Oh, Donner," he breathed, "I'm so glad I didn't share this with you. You most certainly deserve to enjoy the world as you currently know it."

He leaned back and that's when he noticed the jar directly next to his brother's. It had been labeled "Piper Smith."

"What are the odds?" he chuckled.

"You talking about the cure?" the security guard asked, "Yeah, what are the odds that the cure for a disease in the brain is actually poisonous and deadly to the liver and kidneys? The only way to stop the Alzheimer's is to kill the patient."

"Makes you wonder if it's really worth it," Brett muttered, placing a hand on the front of his brother's jar.

"From what you've told me, sounds like he's been having a blast these past nine years."

Brett nodded, then stood up, "I bet he wouldn't trade it for the world."

EPILOGUE

"If I had it all to do over again…"

Yeah, it's one of those questions that come up now and then. Now, as I read the message from my brother informing me that he has found the funding necessary to keep this project going on for at least another half century, it begs that question. I've just had the best ten years of my life and now I was faced with at least fifty more with the woman I love. I'll never tire of this place and I'll never tire of her.

If I had it all to do over again, well, I wouldn't change a single thing. I think I'd seriously jump into that lake in Akron all over again. I honestly do.

Is that crazy?

THE END

Check out these other affordable books available for your Kindle by Scott McElhaney:

The Ani Maxima Files Collection

Selenocentric

Maelstrom

Endeavor

Terraformer

Indentured (Mystic 1)

Legacy (Mystic 2)

Violation (Mystic 3)

Judgment (Mystic 4)

Convergence (Mystic 5)

The Mystic Saga Omnibus (all 5 books)

Warrior of the Myst

Dominion

Vestige

Erinyes

Ghosts of Ophidian

Alastair (Ghosts of Ophidian)

Daylight in Blossom

Beyond the Event Horizon

Mommy's Choice

Elusive December

One Crazy Summer

Talking to the Moon

Saving Brooksie

The Wisconsin Samurai

Made in the USA
Middletown, DE
20 December 2018